Redemption

The Art of D/s Rewritten Prequel

REDEMPTION

ELLA DOMINGUEZ

Redemption

The Art of D/s Rewritten, Prequel

Originally titled The Art of Redemption
First Edition 2014, Art of D/s Series
Copyright Ella Dominguez 2012-2017
Rewritten Edition 2017
All rights reserved

The Art of D/s © Ella Dominguez 2012-2016
The Art of D/s Revised © Ella Dominguez 2013
The Art of D/s Rewritten © Ella Dominguez 2016

This book is a work of fiction. Any resemblances to actual persons, living or dead, events or places are entirely unintentional or coincidental. Names, characters, places and incidents are either the product of the author's imagination or are used fictitiously.

No part of this book may be reproduced, scanned or distributed in any printed or electronic form without written consent of the copyright owner.

ISBN 1539428145
ISBN 10: 1539428141

REDEMPTION

Dedication

To the two loves of my life: my daughter and hubs. They keep me happy, healthy and content, their humor and discipline keep me smiling and in line (most of the time).

REDEMPTION

Acknowledgements

To the loyal readers of the original Art of D/s Trilogy who urged me to write this and wanted the continuation of Isa's and Dylan's story. I will be forever grateful for your encouragement and support.

To my beta readers who are patient, speedy and have the keenest eyes this side of erotica. THANK YOU!

An enormous amount of gratitude goes out to Rebekka Ivàcson for allowing me to use her images throughout the original Art of D/s Trilogy and the reboot, The Art of D/s Rewritten. She is talented beyond belief and I wish her only success & happiness in her life.

REDEMPTION

ELLA DOMINGUEZ

Long Story Short

Previously titled: <u>The Art of Redemption: The Art of D/s, #0.5</u>. Can be read before The Art of D/s Rewritten Trilogy (Submission, Domination, Control), but contains mild spoilers.*

Warning: Contains mild BDSM and situations that may trigger past memories of abuse. Intended for adult readers aged 18+

For Isabel, art is her one saving grace from a life of cruelty and abuse. Bored with conventional sex and unfulfilling relationships, she looks to her own creativity to find an outlet for her secret desires. Introverted, self-critical, yet spirited, she yearns for love, acceptance, and control.

For Dylan, the answer to his control issues and sadistic fantasies waits for him within the walls of the Dark Asylum. Seeking redemption for his overwhelming guilt and sadness over the loss of his parents, he immerses himself completely in the worlds of art and BDSM with voracious passion.

Beginning on the night of the fated Studio 210 gallery show that steers Dylan toward the love of his life, this prequel highlights the years prior to meeting his soulmate and own little artist with a hidden dominant streak—*Mistress Isabel*. That very same night forever changes Isabel's future, as well, and leads her to the man who will capture her heart, dominate her world, and ultimately give her complete control.

REDEMPTION

ELLA DOMINGUEZ

DEDICATION	5
ACKNOWLEDGEMENTS	7
LONG STORY SHORT	9
CHAPTER ONE	13
CHAPTER TWO	21
CHAPTER THREE	27
CHAPTER FOUR	35
CHAPTER FIVE	43
CHAPTER SIX	49
CHAPTER SEVEN	57
CHAPTER EIGHT	65
CHAPTER NINE	71
A GLIMPSE INTO SUBMISSION	79
MORE FROM ELLA DOMINGUEZ	101

REDEMPTION

Chapter One

Dylan

*L*ong legs draped over a man's shoulders. Hands bound in rope across a woman's belly. The man's face rendered indecipherable by a smudge of acrylic paint the color of the Atlantic Ocean.

Every last detail of the painting Dylan was looking at was a goddamn beautiful sight. The bright overhead lamps bathed not only the image but the room with light, banishing the shadows and making all the glorious details of it pop. The artist's name scribbled at the bottom: *Constantine.* Dylan had never heard of him, but what he was looking at was worth far more than the price tag attached to it.

His eyes zoomed in on the bindings around the woman's wrists and an inexplicable sense of curiosity surged through him. *If only he could experience that kind of power over a woman.* He laced his fingers together behind his back and his gaze shifted from the obscured face to the rope again. There was certain *je ne sais quoi* about the work of art. Without a doubt it was erotic, but it was more than that—it was *intriguing,* even *inspiring.*

He reached out and touched the corner of the canvas with loving finesse. The sensation of another person's eyes on him caused a rush of heat to creep up his neck at being caught finger-fucking the artwork.

"Are you into this sort of thing?"

A female's soft yet commanding voice interrupted what should have been a quiet moment of reflection. It wasn't often he got a day off from work, and having just gotten back from eighteen weeks of field training, all he wanted was to spend his twenty-third birthday in peace and fucking silence. He was too mentally and physically exhausted to socialize or put on pretenses of civility.

He stared ahead, his arctic-blue eyes scanning the image once more as he answered blandly, "What do you think? I'm in an art gallery looking at art …"

Her response came quickly and cut his answer short. "I wasn't referring to the art."

"I know what you were referring to," he replied coolly without facing her.

"So, are you?"

Irritated with her persistence, he turned his head and lifted a condescending eyebrow. When her slender form came into view, he adjusted his stance and attitude, but only slightly. She was at least ten years his senior. Not that age mattered. She was gorgeous, though not in the usual way that he found attractive. Her allure appealed to him much more than the young, immature women he was accustomed to spending his time with.

She was tall, and with four-inch heels, she stood eye-to-eye with him, her espresso-colored irises riveted on him. Her dark hair was neatly braided down her back, and the scent of her expensive perfume tantalized his senses. While her figure suggested that she was a woman who worked out frequently, her skin tone revealed she was someone who enjoyed basking in the warmth of the sun. As his eyes roamed over her body, he couldn't help but wonder what color lingerie she was wearing underneath her conservative black, pin-striped skirt and button-down white shirt. That is, if she was wearing any at all.

The corners of her lips curled upward into a smile and she appeared pleased with herself. Although her looks were appealing, there was something about her expression that irked Dylan. He couldn't put his finger on what that *something* was, except to say that her arrogance matched his own, and perhaps it was because facing her was like looking into a mirror.

The question she had asked and repeated was still lingering in the air when she reached into her wristlet, pulled out a business card and slipped it into the pocket of his blazer.

A secret smile formed on her lips. "If you ever get the urge to try what's on that painting, stop by the Dark Asylum. Monday's are open to the public. Tell Kerian that Catalina sent you."

With that, she gave him one last silent examination, starting at his eyes and moving downward. When her eyes came to rest on the crotch of his pants, the corners of her cherry-red lips lifted upward and her face lit up.

"I do hope you find the time to stop by."

As she walked away, he became entranced with the sway of her slim hips and the click of her heels on the concrete floor. He had just been eye-fucked and propositioned, though he wasn't sure what he had been propositioned for.

His fingers found the card in his pocket and plucked it out. He didn't recognize the name of the club or the address, but that didn't surprise him. He wasn't exactly a *clubbing* type, nor did he socialize to a great degree. When he wasn't working, most nights were spent jacking off to online porn or hooking up with anonymous women.

Flipping the card over, he read the inscription.

Experience the ultimate power and release of domination & submission. Private, members only BDSM & fetish club.

His pulse suddenly began to pound in his veins. *Domination and submission.* He had seen the images of such things, even read about them in passing, but to experience it? His cock hardened and his eyes darted around the room, as if he was going to get caught with his hand in the cookie jar.

He took a quick look at the painting again before waving a gallery representative over. Monday was two days away, and two was days too long to wait as far as he was concerned. Until then, he would need something or *someone* to keep him occupied.

When the salesperson approached him, she gave him a playful smile and began blabbering on about the artwork in question. He didn't need the particulars. It spoke to him and that was all that mattered. He feigned interest and gave her his best sexy grin, allowing it to spread across his youthful face and reflect in his lusty blue eyes.

When she turned away, he pressed his fingertips firmly into the small of her back before placing his hand on the curve of her waist to pull her closer. It was a bold and arrogant thing to do, but he had a tendency to be that way when it came to women, and more frequently than not, he unintentionally overstepped his boundaries. Her breathing quickened and when she peeked over her shoulder at him, the heat of excitement stained her cheeks pink. When her tongue slicked across her upper lip and she flashed her come-hither eyes his way, he knew she had accepted his unspoken invitation.

A flicker of satisfaction crossed his face and his eyes grew openly pleased. He had found his plaything for the night, and he'd hardly put any effort into it.

*

Isabel

Taking a mental inventory, Isa recalled all the things she had placed in the small duffle bag that was hidden in her locker—four pairs of jeans, the same number of shirts, a handful of undergarments, and her sketch journal. The rest would come later. Each item had been carefully transferred to school over the last several weeks and secretly stashed away in preparation of her escape. Except for the journal, it was all brand new and paid for with her tutoring money, as she didn't want any of her belongings tainted by her father's touch or money.

Nervous energy pumped through her veins as she counted out, for the third time, the cash she had been saving for just over a year. Sixteen hundred dollars and change was the sum total she possessed to start a new life. She prayed it was enough. *It had to be.*

The sound of her father's footsteps on the stairs made her body tense up with fear. Quickly, she stuffed the cash under her mattress. Just as she grabbed a nearby French language book and hid behind it, the door to her bedroom flung open and the stench of her father's cologne drifted in. She could feel his cold stare boring into her from the other side of the hardbound book, but she didn't dare lift her eyes to him.

She hoped there wouldn't be another beating this night. Not so soon after the last one. Without warning, he lunged at her, tore the book from her hands and tossed it to the floor. The bed dipped next to her as he pinned her down on the bed by placing a knee in her pelvis and his forearm against her throat. When she closed her eyes and turned her face away from him, he forced the full weight of his body onto his arm, cutting off her airway.

"You think I don't know what you're up to?" he breathed against her cheek.

Her pulse pounded erratically in her temples as she became breathless. Her body began to ache under his heavy weight, but she forced herself to lie quiet and motionless as she tried to hold her breath. Her inner voice was screaming at her to scratch his eyes out and knee him in the balls, but she knew better. She had learned at a very young age that if she attempted to fight him, her punishment would only be worse in the end.

"Open your eyes, you little whore, and answer me," he barked, letting up only slightly to allow her to breathe.

Doing as she was told, she pried her lids open to face him and inhale a deep breath of air. The pitch-black, murderous stare focused on her nearly made her retch with fear. This last year had been, by far, the worst for her. His punishments were becoming dangerously more severe with each passing day, and his resentment and hatred toward her was at an all-time high. She knew if she didn't get out now, she would never make it out alive.

He had already tried once to kill her, but rather than taking her life, another trip to the hospital and one more lie about an *accidental* fall down the stairs revealed he had taken the lives of her future unborn children instead. How many more visits to the hospital would it take until those people figured out what was going on in the home of the respected businessman Emilio Ibanez? How many more broken bones and bruises did she have to bear until they would stop looking the other way? What would it take for justice to be served? Tears filled her eyes because she knew the answer without speaking. *Her death.*

When an errant, hot tear that was hovering on her lashes rolled down her cheek, a sinister grin spread across his merciless, wrinkled face. Moving suddenly, he shifted his position and his hand was now around her throat, squeezing the life out of her.

"When will you learn that your fucking tears mean nothing to me?" he hissed as he clamped around her throat tighter.

She had come to that realization long ago, but the tears still came unbidden. Spots filled her vision, and her self-preservation instincts kicked in. She no longer cared what he did to her if she fought him. Clawing at his hands, she thrashed her head and mewled, but the darkness that was hiding in the shadows moved in and an ice-cold sensation wrapped itself around her weakened body. Only then did Papa release her and deliver a slap across her face to bring her out of the impending blackout spell. The heat on her cheek brought her back to reality, and she gasped for breath as she lay beneath him, staring up at him frightened and angry.

He really was trying to kill her.

"Tell me," he ground out gritted through gritted teeth, but she shook her head.

It was her hope that he was only calling her bluff about being up to something. He liked to play this twisted little game of *will you confess to something you haven't done* in an attempt to make up some reason to beat her senseless. Just as she closed her eyes again, she heard the familiar sound of his belt being unbuckled and being pulled from the loops of his pants. *Not this again.* Her body was still hurting from the last time Papa's leather had its way with her.

Thinking quickly, she dared to speak. "Not tonight, Papa," she squeaked out, her vocal cords sore from his assault. "Graduation is tomorrow. People will see the marks."

REDEMPTION

Cursing under his breath, he stood, and just as quickly as he had appeared, he was gone. When she heard his heavy footsteps descend the stairs, she breathed a sigh of relief. It wasn't often she was able to talk him down, but when she did, she felt a prevailing sense of accomplishment.

With her body trembling uncontrollably, she hugged herself and hid her face in her pillow, soaking it with tears. As she let out a deep racking sob, she reminded herself that in less than twenty-four hours, she would be free of him. *Forever.* No more cruel words. No more iron fists. No more Emilio Ibanez. As soon as that diploma was in her hands, she was leaving Georgia and never looking back.

Chapter Two

Dylan

An entire weekend was too long to wait. Dylan had never been a patient individual, and every passing minute seemed to tick by slowly as his anticipation grew for Monday. When it finally arrived, his nerves nearly caused him to back out, but his curiosity was far too great to allow that to happen.

Arriving at the Dark Asylum, he was handed a waiver form and agreement of confidentiality to sign before being allowed entry. He read it over carefully twice before penning his name. It all seemed legitimate and surprisingly well-written. As he entered the main communal area, the scents of oil and leather immediately struck him. It was like no other place he had ever seen. He inspected his surroundings thoroughly, his mind racing. He had no idea what an establishment of this nature was supposed to look like, but he was pleasantly taken aback at the mysterious yet welcoming ambiance.

A tap on his shoulder caught his attention, and a man nearly his height made it known that he was the club owner, Kerian. The man's dark eyes looked him over suspiciously as Dylan promptly introduced himself and stated who had referred him.

"We get a lot of curious young individuals in here, Mr. Young, but this isn't a playground, and I'm not a babysitter. I want to be absolutely clear about something: tonight you're only allowed to watch. Feel free to ask as many questions as you'd like, but if you're in any way disrespectful, or try to engage any of the women physically, you'll be asked to leave and never be allowed back."

REDEMPTION

Dylan's mouth parted in surprise. He wasn't the type of person to act immaturely and frankly, he was offended that just because of his age, Kerian would assume such a thing. He had been taking care of himself for nearly seven years, and he didn't need a fucking babysitter. He took in a deep breath as they stood toe-to-toe, and swallowed his pride while reminding himself that it wasn't personal. Anyway, he wasn't about to leave just yet. Not when his curiosity was piqued at the sound of a woman's screams heard emanating from the back room.

"I understand," he relented through gritted teeth.

"Good. I hope you find my little club pleasurable. So, what fetishes interest you?"

The question perplexed him. Though the thought of bondage had always appealed to him, he wasn't *into* anything except art and getting laid whenever possible.

Not quite sure how he should respond, he shrugged his shoulders and confessed, "I've always liked the idea of tying a woman up."

Kerian nodded and gave Dylan his first smile. "You'll see plenty of that here."

After being introduced to his designated tour guide and being politely reminded to keep his hands to himself, his mouth shut during a scene and to hold all questions until it was over, he was led back further into club and to the area from which the disquieting sounds were originating.

Faced with a small, masked man wielding a flogger against the very woman who had given him the card, Dylan's mouth gaped open in astonishment. Sexual arousal burned low in his gut and worked its way toward his groin. He tried to talk his dick out of stiffening, but it was no use. Tangled emotions surged through his head and heart. On one hand, he wanted to jump in and save the damsel in distress; however, she looked as if she was in anything but distress. In fact, she looked to be quite enjoying it. Even more prevalent was his feeling of jealousy for not being the one responsible for her state of arousal.

Unable to decide whether or not what he was feeling was wrong or right, he instead allowed himself to imagine that he was on the one on the giving end of the lashing.

A glistening sheen of sweat covered the nearly-nude woman as moans of delight slipped past her lips, every sound causing his heart to hammer in his chest and his shaft to become fully erect. Forcing himself to redirect his attention, Dylan eyed the other patrons in the room and studied their expressions. Shadows on the wall danced to the flickering flames from nearby candles. making it difficult to discern the others' faces, but from what he could see, they were all just as mesmerized and turned-on as he was, which helped to put him at ease.

The shrouded man laid down the leather implement and worked his stubby fingers over Catalina's body while whispering into her ear. Dylan moved closer, dying to know the words being spoken, but all at once he felt a firm hand on his shoulder halting him.

Kerian had snuck up on Dylan and was now keeping a close eye on him as he spoke over his shoulder. "Someday you'll get your turn."

Someday wasn't good enough. Dylan wanted to know everything there was about this place and the goings-on *now*. He yearned to be educated on how to use the flogger, the whips and all of the things hanging on the wall just within view.

The ultimate power and release of domination and submission.

He needed to experience what was written on the card that turned out to be the best birthday gift anyone had ever given him.

Watching as the man removed Catalina's shackles, her question popped into his head: *are you into this sort of thing?*

No, he wasn't, but he wanted to be.

*

Isabel

As Isabel walked briskly to the bus station, her anxiety was making it nearly impossible to focus on anything except each step in front of her. With her duffle bag slung over her shoulder, she approached the ticket booth.

"Where to?" the woman behind the glass asked.

"The furthest place I can go one-way on three hundred dollars."

The woman typed on the computer and gave her a number of options. She pondered for a moment while nervously glancing over her shoulder, fearful she would see her father coming to snatch her away and drag her back home to face his cruel wrath. She had never been to any of the places mentioned, but one was as good as another, so long as it was a thousand miles away from Papa.

With her ticket in hand and seated on a long bench, she waited for her bus. Reaching into her coat pocket, she dug out her diploma and read it over again just to make sure it was real. There had barely been enough time to steal her birth certificate, and she had almost been caught in the act of trying to do so. Luckily, she had managed to get her hands on it, as well as her social security card and stuffed it away in her pocket, too.

A large bus outside screeched to a halt and when she heard her boarding number, she wasted no time getting on. Only when the bus was in motion and the lights of Atlanta were no longer in sight did she allow herself to finally relax. Tears of joy filled her eyes, and for the first time since she was a child, she genuinely smiled—the sensation foreign on her lips.

She was really free of her father, and with Atlanta an already fading memory, Denver would be her new home.

REDEMPTION

Chapter Three

Dylan

An intense background check and several rounds of interviews were required of all applicants to the Dark Asylum, and Dylan was no exception. He had waited more than a month since his first visit to the club to start his training to be a Dom. Six unbearably, fucking long weeks to be exact, until someone became available to show him the ropes, so to speak.

And that *someone* was going to be none other than Kerian. He had lucked out that his originally-assigned mentor had been unable to work him due to a family emergency and that the well-respected and long-time Dom and slave owner would be sharing his wisdom. When Catalina volunteered to be his 'learning sub,' he felt he had really hit the jackpot.

Every spare moment in the waiting weeks had been spent at the club, watching and taking mental notes on everything he was seeing and overhearing. Like a sponge, he soaked it all up. All of the Dominants, both men and women, exuded the kind of prowess and power that he longed to possess himself. And the submissives... *hot damn.*

As he recalled the first time he met Catalina, he remembered thinking she had come off as smug, but what he had mistaken for arrogance was simply confidence. Not only were she and the women at the club beauty-personified, but they all radiated a kind of physical awareness of their own bodies and sexuality that was stunning to bear witness to. Their self-assurance, yet meek and subservient attitudes were something he had been attracted to since getting his first taste of pussy.

His nights away from the club were no longer spent as wasted time jerking off to porn and seeking out his next lay, but instead doing online research and reading everything he could about the BDSM lifestyle. It had become his new obsession, and other than art, there was nothing else in his world that captured his attention quite so completely.

As he stood at the back of a crowd watching an intense double-penetration scene that was taking place behind a pane of privacy glass, he heard Kerian's whispered voice over his shoulder.

"One of the most beautiful things in the world is to share something that belongs to you with someone who will cherish it as much as yourself."

Dylan supposed that was true enough, though he wasn't fond of the idea of sharing *anything*, let alone something as precious as a woman. Call him greedy, but he didn't give a shit. If he ever had his own submissive, he sure as hell wasn't going to be loaning her out. It would have to be one special person for him to ever consider doing such a thing.

Then again, it was thrilling to imagine having a woman so completely under his control and command that she would do anything or *anyone* he told her to. His cheeks heated at his wicked thoughts, but he quickly shook off his hesitation. He hadn't learned much about this way of life yet, but he knew enough to realize that nothing was considered too taboo.

Guiding Dylan away from the scene, Kerian walked him over to a secluded area of the club. With Dylan seated in a high-back, black velvet chair, Kerian sat across from him with one leg crossed over his knee as he gave him an intense, quizzical look.

"What are you afraid of, Mr. Young?"

The question momentarily stunned him. He was afraid of a lot of things. Like the unknown, or people finding out about the events surrounding his parents' deaths. Sitting up straight, he puffed his chest out.

"I'm not afraid of anything."

Kerian's fingers curled around the stem of a wineglass filled with ice water that sat on a nearby table. Bringing the goblet to his mouth, he peered at Dylan over the edge as his eyes darkened.

"Everyone has fears," he stated bluntly, as sipped on the water and set it back down. "To not face them, or at minimum, acknowledge them, is not only detrimental to your mental health, but it puts everyone on whom you are exerting your dominance, at risk. Knowing your fears means knowing your limits. It's the very thing we teach submissives."

Dylan rubbed his hand across the nape of his neck and let out an agitated sigh. He had answered the way he thought he was expected to. He thought Doms were supposed to be fearless and unflinching. He thought …

Kerian stood and his thoughtful expression turned to a frown. Crossing his arms over his chest, he shook his head. "Maybe you're not ready for this."

Dylan whipped his head up and glared at him. "I *am* ready," he spoke firmly.

Kerian's long, blunt fingers stroked his chin as he regarded Dylan carefully.

Disappointment at the thought of being denied training to become a Dom squeezed the air from his lungs, and each passing second he sat under Kerian's critical stare felt like a lifetime.

"Men your age make dreadful Doms," Kerian said in a low, composed voice. "They're too focused on how much pussy they can get to see the whole picture, or understand the responsibility of the title. But this lifestyle isn't just about *you* and *your* sexual needs, Mr. Young. If you have any intentions other than being completely honest with me and the submissives who are entrusting you with their safety, then it's best you either wait until you're mature enough to handle the responsibility of being a Dom, or focus your efforts on something else."

Dylan stood in protest. "I've been making my own decisions and living on my own since I was sixteen. I may not have the maturity of a man your age, but I'm neither a child nor is my way of thinking juvenile. I know I can come off as arrogant and self-obsessed, but that's not who I really am on the inside." He bit his bottom lip as he tried to formulate what he was feeling into words. "I want this and not just for the pussy."

Kerian lifted a skeptical eyebrow and tightened his arms over his chest as if calling bullshit.

"Okay, *yes*, the pussy plays a significant part in why I want this, but it's not the *only* reason." Seemingly getting nowhere with Kerian, he threw his hands up in defeat. "Damn it, I *am* ready for this. I've never been more ready for my life to mean something more than right now."

Tossing himself into the chair again, he stared at his hands despondently. "I *need* this."

Letting out a deep sigh, Kerian placed his hand on Dylan's shoulder. "I still don't think you're ready, but I would love for you to prove me wrong. So, I'll ask you this only once more: *what are you afraid of?*"

Dylan let out the breath he had been holding in and relief swept over him. He lifted his head, and his gaze shifted from Kerian's face to a spot on the wall behind him. It had taken years to build up his tough façade and he hated being exposed and forced to explain himself, but he knew if he didn't, the thing he wanted most would be denied him. Gritting his teeth until his jaw creaked, he forced out the words that had lodged in his throat.

"I'm afraid of failure."

And of being alone. Those words he refused to say out loud. No one ever need know that bit of truth about him. *No one.*

*

Isabel

A touch of phthalo blue here, a splash of fawn yellow there, and a smudge of dark magenta just so.

The brush in Isabel's hand glided over the canvas as she created her first painting in her new apartment. The hanging light in the closet pierced the shadowed corners, brightening the tiny space that she had designated as her painting room. The colors on the work in progress were bright and reflected her mood. It was such an odd, exhilarating feeling to be able to paint freely and without fear of hearing her father's footsteps making their way to her.

Looking over her shoulder and out the closet door at the window in the distance, her eyes squinted when she smiled. Her first month's rent was due and the feeling of complete independence filled her. The feeling of bliss was an added bonus to her newfound freedom, and her efficiency apartment, though small and in a less-than-desirable neighborhood, was her own space. This was *her* home. This was *her* life. She wasn't sure what happiness felt like, but with her creativity flowing in abundance, she suspected this was as close to it as she had ever been.

She had been fortunate to secure a job at a bookstore located right on a public transportation route, only days

REDEMPTION

after having moved to Denver, and her landlord had agreed to break up her deposit into three payments so that she could buy some necessities for her new abode. She was also blessed that a friendly older neighbor had given her a few used items of furniture to start out, such as a chest of drawers and a small table with two chairs. And it seemed that luck was with her once again when she found a tiny loveseat on clearance at a furniture store that was going out of business.

Her entire life had been spent praying to a god she doubted was real, but for the first time, she actually felt as though a higher power was really watching out for her. For the first time, she felt safe.

It wasn't until she fell asleep that her ghosts came to haunt her. In her nightmares, it was always her father's eyes on her and his words tearing her down, reminding her that she would never amount to anything, that she was just a stupid, talentless little slut. Always, it was his leather searing across her back and his fists in her diaphragm or a knee in her pelvis. Over a month had passed, and still those dreams and memories were as fresh as the green summer grass growing outside. The happy images that she painted were continually interspersed with dark ones.

When she woke the following day from a particularly horrible dream after hearing her loud neighbors fighting, her body was damp with sweat and tears were running down her cheeks. On this day, there would be no bright paint on her canvas.

As she lay on the floor of that small apartment, she found it hard to rise and to tell herself the things that would normally bring her out of a funk. Papa's murderous eyes kept flashing behind her closed lids, and she knew that no matter how many miles she put between them, no matter how much time passed, she would never truly be free of him. As much as she wanted the images of sexual bondage she painted to become reality, they were only a metaphor for how she felt—forever bound to her father's cruelty. And she knew, without a doubt, that he would eventually come for her. It could be tomorrow or a decade from now, but he would come. And no matter how much joy there was in her life, he would destroy it, along with everyone she cared for.

REDEMPTION

Chapter Four

Dylan

Dylan's weeks of practicing with the flogger on the back wall of the Dark Asylum were over. Tonight was the night he would test it on Catalina's flesh under the watchful eye of Kerian. Standing in front of the mirror in the men's room, he leaned over the sink and stared at himself. Other than shorter hair, he looked exactly the same as he did before his training began. His eyes were the same unusual color of blue, his physique no stronger, no weaker—yet he felt *different*. Scanning his face once more, he tried to put his finger on what it was that felt out of the ordinary.

Was he kinder? A little. *More respectful?* Yes, though he was still learning the importance of that sentiment toward his fellow man and for the women who were freely giving their submission to him. *Was he smarter?* In regards to BDSM, definitely. *So, why was he feeling so damned different?*

Kerian poked his head into the restroom. "Are you having second thoughts?"

Hell no, he wasn't having second thoughts. He shook his head and straightened himself up.

Pushing forward, he followed Kerian to the staged area where Catalina was already waiting. They had grown into a comfortable routine where she would explain her limits and what she hoped for out of the scene. Their encounters had been strictly limited to sensation experimentation on both their parts and only light sexual contact up until that point, but Dylan was hoping for *more* tonight.

REDEMPTION

His nerves prickled with anticipation when Kerian brought a new flogger over to him, one that he had never seen before.

"I had this made for you. At the risk of sounding sentimental, I give this to you with the hopes that you can go forth and become the man I know you were meant to be. Keep in mind your limits and fears, listen to that inner voice even if it's not making sense at that moment, and remember, Dylan, just like in life, there is no failing in BDSM. There is only learning from your mistakes and making right what you've wronged."

No sincerer statement had ever been spoken to him, since his last conversation with his father, and a lump formed in his throat. If only his parents could see the man he had become—the man he was growing into.

Confidently, he took the flogger from Kerian's hands and ran his fingers over the braided leather handle. It was smooth and soft like Catalina's skin, and the smell of new leather exhilarated him. He stepped back and swished it at his side and against this own thigh. The unbroken firmness of the leather strands caused a sting on his own flesh, piquing his arousal.

Walking slowly to Catalina, he allowed her to touch it and to smell it as he pulled his fingers through her long hair. He placed the braided handle between her teeth and spun her around to pull her hair back and away from her face. With her brown locks neatly knotted behind her head, he fettered her wrists and attached them to a long hook on a chain that hung from the ceiling. With her hands high above her head, he turned her back around to face him and noted her dark eyes growing excited as he reached for the flogger.

"I'm one lucky son-of-a-bitch to have met you," he breathed into her parted lips as he leaned down to kiss the corner of her mouth. "Every training Dom should have a Catalina Angelis in their life." Her smile radiated from her glistening lips to her sparkling eyes. "Thank you, Cat, for sensing in me what I didn't have the experience to figure out myself. Thank you for giving me this opportunity," his words lowered to a mere whisper, "and for giving yourself to me so freely and accepting what I'm about to do to you."

She bowed her head in acquiescence and her cheeks turned the most amazing hue of pink he had ever seen.

"It's been my pleasure, Sir," she spoke softly.

Sir.

The word stunned him into silence, and he momentarily lost his train of thought as goosebumps spread over his arms. No one had called him that before. Not during his brief training and not in life. Suddenly he felt it—the thing Kerian had been speaking of all along—the responsibility that came along with the title of *Sir*, of Dominant, of Master. It was a strange sensation he couldn't quite describe, but felt very much like the first time he felt his cock sheathed by a woman's pussy. In a sense, he was losing his virginity again.

As he watched Catalina's body sway hypnotically, he became entranced in her submission. He could hurt her if he wanted. He could even simply just fuck her, but he wanted more than that. He wanted to command her and to control her. And he would.

Taking a predatory stance in front of her, he swirled the flogger in circles around and around until her eyes became glassy. Closing his eyes and circling his head around, his neck cracked loudly. This was it. *This was really fucking it.*

With the first swing of the leather and contact with Cat's tanned, supple flesh, he knew that what he was doing was what he had been meant to do all along. He

REDEMPTION

had waited his whole life for this feeling, and now faced with it, his brain became dizzy with lust.

As he reddened and welted her flesh, he could feel the physical transfer of power just within his reach. Emotionally intoxicated and power-hungry, he dropped the flogger to the floor and knelt before her. With his tongue buried in her wet folds and circling around her swollen clit, she began to plead for her release. The feeling of complete authority saturated every molecule of his being. She had welcomed the pain he had given her and was now begging for his permission to come, and it was up to him to give or deny it. He was this woman's god, even if only for a brief moment, and nothing had ever felt more right.

In a dazzling moment of clarity, he realized what was different about him now: he was no longer a mere man; he was a Dominant.

Isabel

The smile on the young man's clean-shaven face and his lusty gray-blue eyes roaming over Isabel's body made the blood rise to her cheeks. As usual, a sense of awkwardness surged through her, and she didn't know whether to smile back, or run and hide. Instead, she stood staring at him with a look on her face much like a deer in headlights.

Denver and its friendly yet eccentric community were still new to her, as were her surroundings. She was barely making minimum wage at the book store, but she didn't need much anyway. Even though she was sleeping on the floor of her apartment, it was still better than living under Papa's thumb. Anyway, she had nearly saved enough to finally purchase a bed. She hadn't heard from her father and had only recently stopped looking over her shoulder for him. The nightmares were still present, but coming less frequently.

When the man approached her, she latched onto a strand of hair for security and began twirling it between her fingers. He was much cuter than any boy who had looked her way back in Atlanta. Not that there were many of those, but ... her eyes unintentionally darted toward the obvious bulge in his pants. Again her cheeks burned bright red. Silently she hollered at herself to get a grip. It's not as if she didn't know men had penises.

All of nineteen-years-old and a virgin—what the hell would she even do with one if she found herself faced with it? Lick it? Suck it? Flick it? Fuck it? *Holy ignorance.* She had no idea how to do any of that with any kind of skill. Hell, she had never even been on a date or been kissed.

REDEMPTION

She immediately made a mental note to buy a book on human sexuality and read up on the finer points of fooling around.

After introducing himself, he moved closer and began shamelessly flirting with her. Though it wasn't something she was accustomed to, it was nice, and she basked in the attention.

"Has anyone ever told you that you have beautiful eyes?"

A shy smile surfaced and she forced herself to respond. "No, but thank you."

"When do you get off work?"

"At six," she whispered, hopeful that he might actually ask her out.

"Perfect. How about we get a bite to eat?"

She prayed by *bite* he meant more than food. Damn it if her face didn't heat up again. She really needed to get that annoying quirk under control.

The moment he was gone, she made a beeline to the health section and found a book on sexual positions. Maybe she was planning too far ahead, but she wanted to be prepared just in case. No boy had ever shown her any attention or spoken so kindly to her. No one had ever asked her out before either, and she wasn't going to let this opportunity pass her by. She had no sooner cracked the spine of the book when her father's voice boomed in her head.

You're nothing but a little whore like your mother. No one will ever want you.

Her eyes darted downward as she scanned herself. Of course, he was right. Look at her. With the wind knocked out of her sails and what little confidence she had all but gone, she slammed the book closed. Yes, she was definitely getting ahead of herself. It was only dinner, after all. If he even showed up.

To her surprise, he did show up, and he did keep his word on taking her out to dinner. Too bewildered to speak, she sat quietly and let him do all the talking, only adding an occasional remark. Her eyes drifted from his face to the window behind him as lightning tore open the sky and rain lashed against the pane. The windows shuddered violently from the gale force winds, and she hugged herself as his soothing voice carried on. The storm that was raging outside didn't compare to the one within her. Outwardly, she may have appeared to be meek and quiet, but on the inside, she felt anything but. Yes, her spirit may have been broken before, but it was on the mend, and she held great pride in herself for having escaped from her cruel maker.

More than anything, she wanted this young man to see who she really was. Actually, she wanted *anyone* to see who she truly was. In her eyes, she wasn't just some abused and shy thing, but a girl, who despite having never been loved, had managed to get away from her psychotic father, and a person who ultimately just wanted a tiny piece of control over her own life and body. She wanted to open up to him like he was so comfortable doing with her. Not about the things she had been through, because God knows she would never tell anyone about the things her father had put her through, or that her mother hadn't loved her enough to stick around. *Who would want to hear about that horrible stuff anyway?* She simply wanted to talk about what she was into, like art. However, she didn't feel particularly keen on sharing the images that were in her head at the moment either.

She listened with great interest while the dark-blonde haired boy named Alex talked about what it was like growing up in nearby Colorado Springs. He spoke of his family with great affection and Isabel felt a twinge of

REDEMPTION

jealousy. She would never know what it felt like to grow up in a happy household. The few fond but fleeting memories she possessed of her mother were overshadowed by her abandonment, and everything after that had been nothing but pain and misery. Although her mother had always been kind to her, so much time had passed since Isabel had felt her touch or heard her voice, that her memories had faded into oblivion. It was probably better that way since the few recollections that remained were tainted by her father's domestic abuse.

She stared at her knotted hands and tried to concentrate on the sound of Alex's voice, instead of the loss of her mother and childhood. There was no point in dwelling on it. All that ugliness was in the past and things could only get better for her. *They just had to.*

Chapter Five

Dylan

Five months of training to be a Dom and Dylan was only now beginning to feel in his element. Work was keeping him busy, and the stress of his job was ever present. The Dark Asylum and the bevy of women who were eager to pleasure him were a welcome diversion. It wouldn't be long until he would be assisting in training submissives and he looked forward to the day when Kerian would allow him to do so. He was still earning the club members' respect, but he valued their opinions. Not having been part of a family in so long, he was struggling to accept them as well, without feeling overwhelmed with guilt over what had happened to his parents.

As his thoughts drifted to the hideousness memories of his mistake, the cargo plane in which he was riding shuddered from turbulence, breaking his miserable reverie. This was only his second actual field assignment and the unwelcome feeling of tension buzzed through his veins. Clutching at the seatbelt over his chest, he caught the gaze of the man in charge of the mission: Sawyer Morrison. His reputation of being a hard-ass, cold-blooded killer preceded him and Dylan watched as the man's dark eyes appraised him and a muscle in his jaw twitched.

He was warned not to piss off the notorious mercenary Sawyer Morrison, but Dylan stared back at him defiantly anyway, unwilling to reveal his unease. When Dylan continued to stare unflinchingly at him, Sawyer tilted his head to one side and gave him a wry, barely noticeable smirk.

REDEMPTION

"You're a cocky little shit, aren't you?" Sawyer's deep voice carried over the noisy jet engine.

Dylan narrowed his eyes in response. "You got a fuckin' problem with me?"

"No, just your agency," he countered casually and without emotion. "But I'm not the one making the ultimate decisions, so it looks like we're stuck with each other. I hope you're as smart as everyone says you are. If not, it's our asses on the line."

Dylan gritted his teeth and looked away. It had always been about *that.* His *smarts,* as the NSA called them. Or that big fucking brain of his, as his dad used to call it. It was the reason *his agency* had hired him in the first place. He had pleaded for years to be allowed to move from behind the desk to field work, and now here he was, getting the same shit from the CIA that he had been getting for years from his coworkers at the NSA. What did he expect, being the youngest of his peers?

What the fuck ever.

"I hope that training of yours is still fresh in your mind, Young. *Young.* How appropriate."

Morrison was relentless, and Dylan glared at him once again. It always came down to his age, and, yes, probably his attitude, too, but it was all he had. What was he supposed to do? Back down and let people walk all over him? Allow them to see the ever-present-fear of being found out for everything that had gone down with his parents? *To hell with that.* If they didn't like who he was or his attitude, they could go fuck themselves.

"Listen, Old Man, my training isn't in question here. If the agency didn't think I could get the job done, then I wouldn't be here."

Morrison's eyes widened in mock astonishment. "Who are you calling *Old Man*? I'm not even thirty yet."

"Oh, yeah? You could've fooled me," Dylan shot back.

"Yeah, you're a cocky little asshole, alright. We'll see how big your balls are when the bullets start flying, Baby Blue Eyes."

Clearly, Morrison was just trying to goad him. When the men around him began to laugh at the verbal sparring match, Dylan puckered his mouth and held his tongue. He wouldn't give any them, or *anyone,* any reasons to laugh at him.

***

Sixteen horrific, bloody hours later, Dylan had nothing but respect for Morrison.

Back on the military plane, he peered out the small window as they ascended. Just above the horizon, dusk filled the hills with purple mist. The scene was beautifully deceiving considering the hell they had just been through. Sinking low into the seat, his body ached with fatigue and he was glad the mission was finally over.

Holy hell, he couldn't wait to be back inside the Dark Asylum with a woman under his command and feeling the effects of his sweet torture from the cat o'nine tails. The sound of the leather against flesh was more relaxing and arousing than anything he had ever experienced in his short life. Then, to be thanked and sucked off after welting her flesh? Christ, what a powerful feeling. It was only behind the doors of Kerian's club that he felt truly in control. If only he had known of such things years ago …

His eyes shifted focus onto Morrison's stressed and worn face before glancing downward at his duty boots. A ray of sunlight filtered in and glinted off the terrorist's blood that was still splattered on them.

REDEMPTION

Wiping the dampness of the Guam humidity off his brow with the back of his hand, Dylan let out a deep sigh of irritation at how inexperienced he had acted during their outing. He had damn near shit his pants at the lethal look in Morrison's brown eyes as he shot a man point blank in the face without so much as flinching at the backsplash. Those actions, however harsh they may have seemed at the time, had saved the lives of not only himself and Dylan, but the men accompanying them. And probably hundreds more innocent civilians, considering what the terrorist had planned. He watched now as Morrison noticed the specks of blood, bent down and rubbed his boots clean with the cuff of his jacket, as if it was just dirt and not another man's brain matter.

Dylan couldn't help but wonder: could he ever be that cold and calculating? When push came to shove, when people depended on him, would he be able to deliver the final blow to someone with as much determination and detachment as Morrison? That's what he'd been trained to do, yet there was a seed of doubt within him that he could actually go through with it. He had been trained in all sorts of ways it seemed—not just in self-defense and how to take a life, but how to be a Dom.

More doubts seeped in. Would he ever be the kind of man that a submissive required? He knew that being given the gift of a woman's submission was more than just about sex. Kerian had driven that point into his head over and over. Was he even man enough to have a submissive of his own? He wanted one. *Or, did he really?* It was such a tremendous responsibility—like his job. The thought of letting down Kerian and the BDSM community was more than he could fathom.

No, he didn't want that responsibility. Not now or any time soon. He would just have to be content in helping to train them. His mind was too cluttered with other things, the most burdensome of which was guilt, to truly focus on any one woman anyway.

He had failed tonight. His immaturity had shown, and he was disgusted with himself. *God, how he hated failure.* All he ever wanted was to succeed at his endeavors; to be the absolute best; he longed to somehow make his parents proud and redeem himself for all that he had caused. His gaze drifted to some far-off place, and his mom's and dad's faces flashed before his eyes.

Goddamn it, why couldn't he just let it go?

Morrison's voice sliced through his self-loathing and answered his unspoken question.

"We've all been where you're at. If it comes down to doing what needs to be done—*when* it comes down to that, you'll find the strength, Young. We all do."

REDEMPTION

Chapter Six

Isabel

Isa woke to the sound of her own heavy breathing. She had dreamt of ropes wrapped tightly around her wrists and of a handsome man touching her face while whispering words of seduction into her ear. She had no idea where the fantasy was coming from, but she didn't question it, she simply rose from bed and began to put it down on canvas.

As she painted the image, the memory of her first clumsy time with sex returned to taunt her with its awkwardness. Although it had been well over a year since that encounter with Alex, she was still mortified at how lame it had been. He hadn't even waited until she was wet before he dry-thrusted into her. There hadn't even been any time allowed for her to get turned on before he came and then scurried out of her life, like a rat that had finished eating a stolen meal.

Even the second man she had been with was a joke in the sack. All the time she had spent reading up on sexual positions post Mr. Two-Pump Chump had been time wasted considering her next lover had been strictly a missionary-position man.

Would sex always be boring and unappealing for her? Perhaps her expectations were too high, but were being excited and aroused asking too much? She had read about the mythical orgasm, but she had yet to experience it herself. Maybe the *Big O* was an urban legend—something men made up to string women along with so they could get into their panties.

Oh hell, with her looks and lack of education, she was lucky any man was interested in getting between her legs at all.

REDEMPTION

Education. She smiled as she laid down another layer of dark blue acrylic paint. Her art class was beginning in only two short weeks. She had been saving her pennies to take the six-week session, and she was excited at the prospect of learning about the classics, while sketching naked men.

The painting progressed nicely as she recalled the previous year and all the dullness of it. It was hard to believe it had been a year and a half since she had made her break from Papa. Time was flying by, and in another six months she would be twenty-one years old. *What then?*

Two hours later, her kinky masterpiece was complete. It wasn't half bad. She grinned and signed her name at the bottom before walking out of the closet and over to a window facing the street.

The silvery moonlight peeked through a dark cloud just long enough to glimmer against the falling snow. In that brief moment of clarity, her eyes scanned the inky night sky beyond in search of a star to make a wish upon, but there were none to be seen. Opening the window, she reached a hand out to feel the flakes against her palm and inhaled a deep breath of crisp winter air. As much as she cherished her freedom, the sting of loneliness was palpable. Would she always feel like this? Would there ever be true love and acceptance in her life? Her amber eyes welled up and the bitter taste of disillusionment whipped through her. She longed for her fairytale ending and for a princely man to save her, but deep down, she knew life was too cruel for such childish fantasies.

Unable to bear children, incapable of understanding or comprehending love, powerless to accept herself... no one could ever care for such a deeply flawed and damaged individual. The dismal thought left her feeling depressed and deeply saddened. She was truly unlovable and her own flesh and blood was to blame.

*

Dylan

Dylan dressed and moved about his bedroom with purpose. Tuesdays and Thursdays were training days and a new batch of wannabe submissives were awaiting his instruction. In particular, there was a leggy, dark-haired temptress he was impatient to sink his teeth into again.

Dressed in his best, most comfortable attire, he readied himself for another night of debauchery and enlightenment.

The drive to the club was filled with thoughts of his upcoming endeavor—starting his own company. He had sought all the legal advice he could and even had his finances sorted in order to get everything underway. The only thing missing: a core of employees that he could trust with his life. In the line of work that he was going into, trust was key and hiring people off the street wasn't an option. He had a few people in mind he wanted to bring on board, but hadn't yet approached them—the first being Sawyer Morrison.

They had kept in touch over the last year-and-a-half and Morrison had proved himself to be an invaluable resource for knowledge and advice. It was strange considering he initially thought the man didn't like him. He would even go so far as to say he considered Sawyer to be his *friend*. Reality struck him full force when he came to the conclusion that Sawyer was, in fact, the only person he considered to be a true friend and someone he could share his secrets with.

When they had last spoken, Morrison had stated he was taking leave to care for his cancer-ridden wife, and

Dylan's heart had ached for him. He didn't know a great deal of personal information about Morrison, but he knew that Sawyer didn't have anyone else in his life or any other family to speak of. It was part of the reason that Dylan felt a connection with him. Just as he parked his car, he felt the urge to speak with Sawyer and check on his well-being.

As soon as Morrison answered the phone, Dylan could hear the liquor in his voice.

"She's gone, Young."

Sawyer's husky, distressing tone and words washed over Dylan in waves. He knew too well the feeling of loss, yet he had no words of sympathy to give him except for, "I'm so sorry, Morrison."

"She's really fucking gone. Now what am I supposed to do?" he suddenly broke into deep sobs.

Morrison was the most resilient man he knew and to hear his anguish cut through Dylan.

"And the goddamn CIA," Morrison's voice turned cold and harsh. "They said I was a liability. That my drinking... that I'm not worthy to carry their fucking badge anymore. After everything I did for them. After lying to Serena for so many years about what I did for them ..."

Dylan put the key back into the ignition and drove away from the club. Morrison needed him.

When he arrived at Sawyer's condo, the skin around his eyes appeared bruised from his sorrow and tears, and his lids drooped with drunkenness. His clothes were rumpled, and his normally organized and spotless home was a chaotic mess.

After cleaning Morrison up, Dylan put him to bed. Just as he attempted to leave, Sawyer reached a hand out and gripped his wrist. The corners of his glassy eyes tightened in despair.

"I loved her so much, Young. If you ever find someone you love as much as I loved Serena, don't ever lie to her, don't ever hurt her, and don't ever fucking let her go."

His body suddenly went limp with exhaustion and intoxication, and his statement left Dylan reeling. He walked to the window as the words sunk in. Pushing the drapes aside, he stared up at the dark, cloudy and moonless night and watched as the snowflakes whirled around in the wind outside. Finding love had never been on his agenda. How could it be when he was incapable of loving himself? No one in their right mind would ever accept him after what he had done to his parents. And could he blame them? *Fuck no.* He had brought it all on himself.

He waited a few more minutes until Sawyer's breathing deepened before writing him a letter, offering him a job as head of security with his company and leaving it on his bedside table. He hoped Morrison would clean himself up and accept his proposition, or else he had no idea what he would do. There was no one else he wanted as his right-hand man. Fuck the CIA. If they couldn't see the true value in a loyal person like Sawyer, then their loss would be his gain.

It looks like we're stuck with each other.

Sawyer's words that had been spoken in jest couldn't have ended up being a truer statement.

With Morrison resting and the condo cleaned up, Dylan drove through the snow to the Dark Asylum. The pretty brunette named Erica was waiting for him and he was impatient to get his hands on her once more. When he arrived, she made her way from across the room to him and his cock immediately awakened at the ravenous look in her eyes. This would be their fifth time together at the club and he was eager to push her body to the

REDEMPTION

brink again. He had never met a submissive quite like her. She was a bottomless bottom and damn if he couldn't stay away from her.

Except for one small thing, she was essentially limitless. More to the point, she was inexhaustible and boundless. It was an intriguing and frightening concept, and one that he fully intended on putting to the test. With the infinite possibilities of Erica on his mind every waking moment since first meeting her, all the other submissives who were vying for his attention had fallen off his radar.

Erica fucking Lawson. It was hard to think about anything or anyone else. *Hard.* He inwardly laughed to himself because that's exactly what he was as she moved catlike toward him with that hungry, insatiable look in her mahogany eyes. He was hungry, too—hungry to give her the kind of pain that she craved; starving to fuck her in agonizing ways and make her beg for more.

Slowly, she knelt before him and pressed her palm to his groin. "I'd like to offer myself to you, Sir," she tugged the waistband of his pants down to expose his hard cock. Gripping his dick, she squeezed tightly as her hand began to glide up and down. She batted her lashes and stated her objective. "I'd like to be your submissive. Full-time."

Dylan's interest was piqued. He never had any intention of having a full-time submissive. That meant responsibility and caretaking on a whole other level. When he sat quietly contemplating her offer, her grip tightened along the ridges of his shaft.

"I would belong to only you, Sir. I would be yours to do with *whatever* you want. *Whenever* you want."

It was tempting... *so very tempting.*

"No limits, Sir. Nothing is off the table with me. My body for your pleasure—to use and abuse however you see fit."

Goddamn. *No limits.* Save for giving head. But, really, not getting his dick sucked in exchange for everything else he would be allowed to do to her? How could he say no to that? *He would be crazy to say no to that.*

His eyes grew wild at the thought of exploiting and manipulating her body without restriction. If only she would accept his cock in her mouth ... *Fuck it.* Anyway, it's not as if there weren't plenty of other subs who could fill in for Erica when it came to sucking him off.

He could live without getting head from his favorite sub, so long as she could take every other twisted thing he intended on doing to her. Full-time? *Hell yes.* The offer of endless possibilities that he could put this woman through was something he was definitely going to claim for himself.

REDEMPTION

Chapter Seven

Isabel

Isa sat staring at her interlaced fingers, dreading the inevitable. When her latest relationship mistake, Anderson, had left a week earlier, he had drained her bank account dry. She had tried to come up with some way that she could make ends meet, but her paycheck wasn't due for another week and a half, she had no food in her pantry and rent was already a week past due.

How could she have been with such a despicable asshole? Wasn't it enough that he had humiliated her, incessantly put her down and gave her nothing but hell about her artwork? She was happy he was finally out of her life, but now she was being forced to do the one thing she swore she would never do: ask Papa for help.

She picked up the phone and dialed her father's number only to hang up. She couldn't bring herself to do it. It had been four long years since she had spoken to him; four peaceful years not hearing his voice or harsh words. She knew she should've run the other way when Anderson kept sniffing around like a hound in heat, but *no*, she was too damned starved for attention to send him on his merry damned way. If only he hadn't been so persistent.

Holy absurdity, his small pecker hadn't even been worth all the havoc he had wreaked in her life. Nearly a year wasted with his worthless, no-orgasm giving ass. Isa grumbled to herself as she stood and began pacing her apartment floor. There was nothing in her name worth any real value that she could sell except maybe her artwork. *What a laugh.* Who the hell would want to buy her perverted paintings anyway?

REDEMPTION

She pushed her unkind words about her art to the back of her mind and quickly chastised herself for thinking of them in that way. They weren't perverted—they were an honest representation of her desires. They were part of her and who she was. They were all she had that was worth anything, even if the value of them was only held within her heart.

Anderson had tried to stifle her creativity just like Papa had, but he had failed. They both had. That's why Anderson had left. Not because she wasn't really good enough for him like he had said. Or, maybe she wasn't good enough for him. Either way, she didn't care. He was gone and good-fucking-riddance.

But this? To be made to call her father now after all this time? She hoped Anderson's miniscule cock and balls shriveled up and fell off for making her resort to this. It would serve his cheating ass right. She swore to herself if she ever saw him again, she would exact her own version of sweet revenge on him.

Seated on the edge of her bed, she forced herself to do the unthinkable and redialed Papa's number. As soon as his voice came over the other end of the line, it was as if no time had passed between them when he tore into her.

"You must be in a shitload of trouble to be calling after all this time."

Her voice was barely a whisper of a sound when she answered, "Yes, Papa."

When she heard her own childlike tone, she inwardly screamed at herself to be strong. Her mind was frantic with fear and her heart was lodged in her throat, but all she could do was sit motionless like an imbecile and take his abuse like she had done all those years ago. Four fucking years she had lived on her own and supported herself, and she was still the same pathetic little girl who couldn't stand up to him. She wordlessly urged herself to hang up the phone, but she knew he was her only source of help.

Damn that Anderson Hayes.

"What's the matter? Did your whoring ass get pregnant?"

His malicious words lacerated her heart. He knew damned well she couldn't carry a child, and his statement only devastated her further, causing her to slide off the bed and sink to her knees. Her bottom lip trembled but she bit it harshly. The least she could do for herself was prevent him from hearing her torment.

"I need you to send me money." Her stomach roiled at how feeble she sounded.

"I didn't hear a *please* with that, Isa," he laughed acidly under his breath. "Beg, you little cunt."

Damn him. She swallowed her pride and let the words slip past her lips with her eyes tightly closed. "Please, Papa. I need your help." She moved the phone away from her mouth, fearful she was going to vomit.

"Of course you do. You'll always need me and you'll always be just like that slut mother of yours, too; useless, ignorant, and dependent on me."

After giving him her address, she hung up the phone, dropped it to the floor and hugged her body as she began to rock herself. She had no doubt that he would send her the money, but at a cost. Her fragile nerves began to splinter and her mind to shut down. With her lips clamped together, she drew in a deep breath through her nose and coaxed herself to rein in her despair.

Rising from the floor, she stiffly walked to the open window and stared up at the pink and orange globe that peeked over the eastern horizon. A spring breeze blew in, and the brisk morning air caressed her cheek and dried her tears as if telling her that everything was going to be okay. The sunshine streamed through the tree leaves outside and flickered across her floor as a peaceful sensation came over her with the realization that Papa was more than a thousand miles away and couldn't hurt her anymore. His words were all that he had to use against her, and she wouldn't allow him the satisfaction. Not anymore. Not ever again.

*

Dylan

Twenty-one fucking months of lies is all that Dylan's relationship with Erica had turned out to be. *And all for what?* The goddamned money.

As he stared at the Denver cityscape out his lawyer's window, sunlight strained its way past the thick venetian blind and momentarily dazed him. Pushing the shades aside, he focused on a lonely patch of green grass amongst the pavement outside. While his legal counsel explained how they planned to deal with the blackmailing bitch with whom he had entrusted his secrets, he recalled their last ugly meeting.

It was supposed to be a nice dinner out with his favorite masochist, followed by another night of kinky fun. Instead it turned out to be the second worst night of his life, only surpassed by the night he found out his parents were dead.

She had looked good in her tight-fitting, red summer dress, her hair neatly pulled back into a low ponytail and her nipples taut and poking through the light fabric of her frock. He sighed irritably. Yeah, she had made sure she looked good alright while she fucked him over in the worst possible way.

Her lusty brown eyes had shined brightly when she had informed him that she wanted money. His response had been to ask how much while reaching for his check book. He was such an idiot. He had thought she simply wanted to do a bit of shopping, and he was all too willing to give her what she wanted in order to see that sweet smile of hers, a smile that he now knew was nothing but a fucking lie.

A couple hundred thousand should do fine for now, she had answered back.

He must've looked like a complete pussy-whipped piece of shit to her, as he'd sat wide-eyed staring back at her with his pen in his hand.

What are you waiting for? She had coolly asked when he sat staring gape-jawed at her.

Start writing or else I'll tell all of Denver what you're into. How you like to make me have sex with other men in front of you while you jack off. How you enjoy beating the hell out of me and fist-fucking me just so you can hear my screams. I bet the newspapers would love to hear all about that and about what you did to your parents, D.

Holy fucking Christ, she hadn't even batted a lash when she'd torn his heart out.

I can see you're a little flustered. It's understandable given the situation, so I'll give you twenty-four hours to finish writing that check out. I know you like even numbers so, for now, let's go with exactly two-hundred thousand dollars.

She had casually walked away from him and their life together as though none of it had mattered, and what she had just done was like another uneventful day at work. The unemotional expression on her face as she strode away made it perfectly clear to him that he had meant nothing to her, and never had.

But she had underestimated him. He may not have wanted anyone to find out about his sexual proclivities, but he sure as hell wasn't going to allow her to threaten

REDEMPTION

him. He refused to live like that, and he didn't need twenty-four hours to come to that decision. It took him all of two minutes to gather his senses and drive straight to his lawyer's office where they promptly began drafting a notice of cease and desist of all threats and contact, or else charges of conspiracy to defraud and blackmail would be brought against her.

Two hours later, the full brevity of the situation had begun to sink in. Her smart-ass remark about him being *flustered* didn't come anywhere close to an accurate description of his emotions. He was a helluva lot more than merely agitated and nervous. He was at a complete loss for words after everything that had transpired between them.

All of it—lies. He still couldn't believe it. Almost two fucking years wasted with her. He had told her things he hadn't told anyone. He had allowed her into his home to live with him. He had trusted her with his life. She had slept next to him and held him, and all of it was nothing but one huge fucking game of emotional and sexual treason. He may have never loved her, but that didn't take away from the sting of her betrayal.

He belted out a breathy, ironic laugh causing his lawyers to look over at him. Karma was a real cocksucking bitch—unlike Erica Lawson. *No head for nearly two goddamned years?* Jesus, he was an asshole for having let her fuck him over like that and for thinking that he had it made with her. After the stunt he pulled with her parents, it served him right to have his life fucked up beyond repair.

Once at home, he stood outside his dungeon and eyed all of the equipment and tools that he had mastered during his years of being a Dom. He would miss it. Every last bit of it. But most especially the powerful feeling that came with dominating a submissive. Glancing over his shoulder, the spare room door sat ajar.

Erica Fucking Lawson. How could he have been so blind?

A hot tide of inner loathing stung the back of his throat. Sawyer had tried to caution him about her, but he was so damned fascinated with her that he had ignored his warnings. It wasn't necessarily a fascination with her as much as it was a fixation on what she was allowing him to do to her. He had been living out his sadistic fantasies with her and she had always come back for more—even begged for it. All along he thought it was because she enjoyed it, because she needed the pain like he needed to inflict it, that she accepted his actions because she cared about what made him happy, *but no.* It was simply because she wanted what was in his bank account.

Of course she only wanted his money. He was unlovable.

He pivoted on one foot and kicked the door to her room open. All his pent-up anger ripped through him like a firestorm as he began to tear the room apart, shredding everything that his hands came into contact with. His grunts and garbled moans echoed throughout the room and hallway as he destroyed the last of her possessions—belongings he had bought and given to her like a lust-struck jackass.

When he was done ravaging Erica's room, he made his way to the dungeon and to hide everything away underneath fresh linen, and slammed the door closed behind him.

Everything he had known, everyone he had grown close to, the only real family he had, was gone and his life as he knew it was over.

No more BDSM.

REDEMPTION

No more Dark Asylum.

No more hedonistic and sadistic pleasure.

No matter how much he needed those things, he couldn't ever risk someone holding those things over his head and threatening him again.

A sense of obligation to warn the others at the club about Erica crept up on him, but the overwhelming sense of shame hanging over him was more powerful. How could he tell Kerian and the community that he had been too trusting and blinded to see the truth? That his dick had done his thinking for him? That he had been drunk with power and missed the signs? He couldn't.

Seated in his office chair with his elbows braced on his thighs, he held his head in his hands, as he closed his eyes and let his anger seep away. At least he still had art. No one could ever take that away from him. Not even that threatening, backstabbing cunt Erica Fucking Lawson.

Chapter Eight

Isabel

Isa may have had a dream job in an art gallery, but her elation was tempered by a boss from hell who wouldn't keep his hands off of her. She sat staring at her hands as Mr. Greer circled around her like a vulture seeking its prey. His fingers pushed her hair aside and skimmed along the back of her neck sending shivers of loathing down her spine.

God, she hated when he touched her.

Her brain was yelling at her to say or do something to put a stop to it, but as usual, she just sat there like a dimwit and took it. What could she say to him anyway without risking her job and a career that she loved? An occupation that afforded her the luxury of being around beautiful images painted by *real* artists? She had been putting up with his sexual inappropriateness for practically a year now, and with each passing minute, he only got bolder with his advances.

Now here he was, in her apartment. He could have any woman in the office, so why her? Why now? It certainly wasn't because of her *sexual appeal* or looks. Most likely it had to do with the fact that he could bully and dominate her. And she fucking allowed it. Disgusted with herself and unable to take anymore, she rose from her loveseat to demand he leave when he reached into a small bag he had brought along and pulled out a bottle of wine.

She eyed it dubiously, but then reached for it. A drink would ease her nerves and it might even give her the courage to kick his ass out. Just one drink, though. *Only one,* she promised herself.

REDEMPTION

Disjointed sounds, images and sensations came next. Mr. Greer standing over her as his pants slid down his slim hips, his rigid cock coming into view. The ripping sound of a condom wrapper being opened and the snap of rubber. Hot, needy hands squeezing her breasts and slipping inside her panties. His fingers slick with her juices running across her lips. Her clothing being removed piece by piece. A raspy tongue felt on her cheek. A nibble on her neck. A tweak of her nipples and then a mouth in places that hadn't experienced male attention in almost a year.

God, no.

She thrashed and tried to push him away, but her limbs were too thick and heavy. She opened her mouth to voice her objections, but her vocal chords refused to cooperate.

"You taste so good, Isabel," she vaguely heard from between her legs, but the light was too bright in her eyes and her vision too bleary to tell if what was happening was real or imagined.

She prayed it was all just a horrible dream, while knowing that it wasn't.

Hands on her knees pushing her legs apart. Penetration. Grunting. Her body being flipped over and manipulated into uncomfortable positions. A sheen of sweat across Greer's forehead as he pinned her below the weight of his body. His lips curled into a satisfied sneer.

The room around her began to spin, and the dinner and alcohol in her belly rumbled and threatened to spill out of her. When he draped her legs over his shoulders and pushed deeply into her, she gagged.

Struggling to stay lucid, she combated the booze and heard herself pleading with Greer when he hit her cervix. Instead of showing her mercy, she felt more pressure between her legs and heard wet sounds.

"I knew this pussy was worth the wait. I know you want it ... stop begging me."

The words he spoke in his English accent kept seeping into her semi-conscious reality, but she couldn't make sense of them.

Why had she consumed so damned much?

When she awoke eight hours later, she was naked on her couch, and her clothes lay scattered on the floor next to her. The smell of sex and Mr. Greer's aftershave still lingered in the air, causing her to bolt to the bathroom where she vomited violently. She dry-heaved repeatedly until there was nothing left in her stomach and her abdominal muscles ached. She tried to remember the details of what had happened the night before, but it was all a fuzzy memory.

His dick inside of her. That's all she could recollect. That's all she wanted to recall. To think about any of the other ghastly details was too much for her to handle.

Dragging herself to the shower, she washed off all traces of the asshole that had taken advantage of her, and began to sob when the realization of what had happened sank in. She had betrayed her own body by permitting that man inside her home, getting drunk and then allowing him to have his way with her. In turn, her body had betrayed her by giving Greer the impression that she had been aroused by his hands on her.

You're so wet for me, Isa.

Greer's statement sent another wave of nausea crashing over her. With the cool water cascading down her used body, anger raked over her like hot coals. At that moment, she hated herself. If she hadn't drunk so much, this never would've happened. Yes, Greer was culpable for his actions, but in her own eyes, she was ultimately the one to blame. She knew better than to drink. She could've fought him harder. Did she really say *no?* Did that word ever actually come out of her drunken mouth? She had no idea. She was too damned inebriated to remember.

Her father had been right about her all along—she was nothing but an ignorant little slut who didn't deserve love.

*

Dylan

With his heart pounding in his chest and his pulse hammering in his stiff cock, Dylan circled methodically and slowly around the thin, leggy, chestnut-color haired woman hanging from the suspension rig in front of him. As he brought the cat o'nine tails up midair, he slowed his breathing and widened his stance. A shiver of arousal crept up his spine and hardened his cock further when he brought the leather down across her stomach in one swift motion. The sight of her welted flesh and the pained shriek that followed sent power coursing through his veins. Her eyes grew liquid, and her body writhed against the restraints.

It felt so good to be in control again.

The sound of chains jangling overhead lulled him into a relaxed state. Right here, in this moment, he owned this woman. It made no difference who she was, just that she belonged to him—*all of her*—mind, body and soul. With a series of deliberate strokes, he snapped the cat on her upper thighs and then swept the cowhide against her clit in one short burst of fury. With her eyes closed tightly, she screamed his name, and he felt like a god.

Damn, he had missed this.

The cool sensation of pre-come wet the front of his pants and he gripped his shaft, anxious to plunge balls deep into her tight ass.

"Please, Sir, I want that big dick of yours in my mouth," he heard her begging. "Give me more pain... *please.*"

Something off to his right broke his concentration. He tried to ignore the dull buzzing as he began to unshackle the woman in preparation of giving her what they both wanted, but it only got louder.

Buzz.

"Don't leave me, Sir. I want you to fuck my mouth ..."

BUZZ.

"I need the pain that you give me..."

Hell yes, he wanted to fuck her mouth and to feel the tightness of her throat around his cock, but to give her more pain? *Fuck. Yes.* That's what he craved the most.

Chirp.

Dylan pried his eyes open. His sweet moment of ecstasy had only been a dream. Glancing at the side table, his cell phone lit up with a message and Sawyer's name flashed across the screen.

Where was he? His eyes scanned the unfamiliar darkened room and when he sat up he felt the warmth of another body next to him and smelled perfume.

Shit.

He must have unintentionally dozed off after sex with. Unable to remember what the hell her name was, he flipped on the lamp and pushed her dark hair away from her face. Carrie? No. *Fuck, fuck, fuck.* Something that began with the letter C.

He threw the bed sheet aside, slipped out of bed and grabbed his clothes that were strewn on the floor. Just

REDEMPTION

like his dream, it made no fucking difference what the woman's name was. He had gotten what he wanted from her. As he dressed, he shook his head in disappointment. No, he hadn't *really* gotten what he wanted from her. He had simply *gotten off.*

As he dressed quietly, he eyed her nude body once again. It was no wonder he couldn't remember her name; she looked just like all the rest. Hell, she even *fucked* just like all the rest. Boring, vanilla fucks... every single goddamned one of them, all of them with no sense of adventure and without a kinky bone in their fit, toned bodies.

Cassie. That was her name. Just another fucking waste of pussy and another woman to file away with all the rest.

Chapter Nine

Isabel

If it wasn't for her love of all things art-related, Isabel would've quit immediately after her one-night mistake with Greer. Instead, she was being further degraded on a daily basis by his lewd comments and the way he undressed her with his eyes. As if it wasn't bad enough that she had to always look over her shoulder for Greer, Monica, his crony and event coordinator, had it out for her, too. Holy royal bitchiness, that woman needed a good ass-whooping. She would do it too, if only she had a set of balls.

Another charity gallery show was scheduled for the following night and she kept herself busy arranging the various paintings of local artists throughout the gallery floor. As she delicately hung each one with love, her fingers itched to touch the texture of the paint on the canvas, though she knew better. These were prized possessions, the likes of which she was lucky to even gaze upon. What she wouldn't give to have as much talent as anyone of the artists who had painted them. A coworker joined her on the floor and slipped the guest list into her hand.

When she read a few of the names, she was in awe. Monica may have been a bitch, but she sure knew how to put on a good show. Art collectors from all over the U.S. would be in attendance, including a few local ones. Resentment quickly washed away her excitement. She had begged Monica to allow her to be involved in some small way with the festivities during the show, but she had refused. It wasn't because they didn't need the help, either. It was out of spitefulness on Monica's part because she had eyes for Greer.

REDEMPTION

When she was done helping out, she turned to her next task at her desk, when she suddenly felt Greer's eyes on her. Looking up from her paperwork, he was standing directly in front of her with his head tilted to one side. Sexual innuendo oozed off of him as he licked his lips and winked at her. Stroking his palm over his stubbled jawline, he tipped his head back and glared down at her. His mouth parted as if to speak, but Monica unexpectedly appeared and interrupted him, and Isa had never been more grateful.

Once home, she had just begun getting ready for a shower when she heard the door buzzer notifying her that a visitor was calling. Her stomach churned. The only visitor she ever received was Greer. She stared at the intercom, refusing to answer it. She didn't want or need his shit tonight. The buzzer chimed two more times before going silent. Just as she let out a sigh of relief, a knock on her door startled her. It occurred to her that he must've buzzed all the apartments until he was let in. Without making a sound, she stood near the door. If she was quiet enough, maybe he would just leave.

"I know you're home, Ms. Ibanez," she heard from the other side of the door.

Only wearing a towel, she reached for her robe and quickly covered herself before allowing him in. When he pushed past her, the smell of his repugnant cologne floated into the room.

"We had an unexpected sale today," he stated and paused to smile lewdly at her.

Taking one step, he reached his hand out and trailed a finger down the smooth line of her jaw. Repulsed by his touch, she jerked away from him. He chuckled and turned his body away.

"I want to borrow a few of your paintings to fill the blank space in the green room. I'm here to pick them up."

Horrified and panic-stricken, she violently shook her head. "No, you can't. Those paintings aren't meant for anyone's eyes but my own," she blared, as she tightened the strings around her waist.

Greer spun on his heel to face her. His dark eyebrows lowered and the lines around his mouth deepened.

"I *what*? I *can't*? Did you really just say that to your boss?" His nearly six-foot frame, broad shoulders and rugged European face screamed beware, and she quickly backed away. "Anyway," he gave a careless shrug as he moved to her bed and reached for a painting. "I wasn't asking." With his back turned to her, he casually glanced over his shoulder. The edge of his mouth curled into a sardonic grin, and he let out a short, breathy laugh. "I *can't*. Silly, little American girl. I can do whatever the fuck I want."

Isa clenched her hands into fists until her knuckles blanched. *Damn him.* Anger consumed her at his assumption that he could do whatever the hell he wanted. Infuriated, she strode toward him, ready to lunge at him and rip him a new asshole for touching her belongings.

Gathering her courage, she put her hand over his just as he loosened the second piece of art from the wall.

"You're *not* taking those."

A muscle in his jaw twitched. "How thick are you?" he belted out. "Do you want me to tell everyone at work how you got drunk and fucked your boss, or would you rather just lose your job altogether?"

Isa gasped out loud and raised her hand, ready to slap his arrogant mouth for saying such a vile thing.

REDEMPTION

"Do it and see what happens," he growled.

His glacial stare froze Isa in her spot and her hand dropped to her side. *What the hell had gotten into her?*

With three of her paintings in his arms, Greer ambled to the door and turned the knob. Just as the door creaked open, he shot her an aggravated look over his shoulder.

"If you weren't being such a little bitch I wouldn't have had to get shitty with you. I just don't understand why you're making such a big deal about this. It's not like anyone will give them a second glance. You'll get your precious fucking paintings back in a few days. Now cheer the hell up and maybe I'll dick you again later."

Repulsed and enraged, Isa whipped her head around and glared at him. "Just get out," she whispered angrily under her breath.

She watched with unshed tears bordering her lashes as the door closed behind him. When he was gone, she stared out the window and down at the street as he loaded three pieces to the puzzle of her shattered soul into the back of his car.

Trying to get her raging emotions under control, she fought against the tears building at the back of her eyes. It was her own damn fault that Greer thought he could do anything he wanted with her. She should've gone through with her initial reaction to his vile statement and slapped him. He deserved far worse than that after what he had done and said to her.

If only the same strong girl within her would make an appearance in the real world, her life might be easier. Okay, maybe not *easier,* but she sure as hell would be happier for it. He may have been a complete asshole, but he was right about one thing: no one in their right mind would want to look at her wretched paintings. My, God, the subject matter alone was enough to put everyone off.

Again, she rebuked the thought. They weren't wretched, and even if they weren't worth a lot monetarily, they were the only thing of real value that she owned. When she felt alone or afraid, her art was the only thing that gave her solace. Her creativity was the only outlet she had to express her inner desires. It had saved her sanity. Her ability to put down on canvas what was in her mind was the only redeeming quality she had gained from the cruel man who was her father and the woman who had deserted her. So what if those images were considered taboo or erotic? They belonged to her. But, damn it, those paintings were private. She didn't want strangers' eyes looking them over, assessing and critiquing them.

Sinking onto her bed, she lay back and stared up at the empty wall above her before turning onto her side and hugging her knees to her chest. The tears that were lingering in the corners of her eyes streamed down her cheeks and she let out a pitiful sob. She was alone and now her paintings were gone. Despair tore at her heart and she hid her face in her pillow.

No one would ever love her, and no one would ever understand what her artwork meant to her. *No one.*

*

Dylan

With an irritated glance in the mirror, Dylan eyed his appearance. Running his fingers through his dark hair, he pushed it away from his eyes and cursed under his breath. He was badly in need of a woman's company, but having been too busy with work, he didn't have the forethought to invite anyone to the charity art show he was about to attend.

REDEMPTION

He reached into his pocket and touched the invitation. He hoped this show would be better than the previous two.

The drive to the exhibit was long and boring, and his mood was glum when he arrived. He waited in his car, contemplating whether or not to go inside. Outside his car, he could hear the muffled sounds of excited voices as other art collectors and local celebrities arrived, the familiar noise rasped against his fragile nerves. As he sat watching from his car, he could see the usual pretentious assholes milling around inside. The flash of a camera went off on the red carpet only a few feet away as he put his car into drive to leave. Just as he turned the wheel to pull out into traffic, the valet attendant approached him.

Fuck it. He didn't have anything better to do with his time anyway.

He stepped foot inside the gallery, and the brightness of the room highlighting the colorful images nearly blinded him with all the cheerful hideousness. As he checked his watch, he sighed with bitter resentment at what his life had become. *Dull*—in every possible fucking way. The women he encountered—unexciting and without personality; the sex he had—tedious and dreary. The only other thing other than BDSM that used to bring him pleasure had even become lackluster—*his beloved art.*

Only his dreams brought him any kind of joy. There, he could be the man he once was—dominant; powerful; godlike. While he slept, he was still King of his Domain. Only the occasional reappearance of *her* in his dreams jacked with his sleepy calm.

Rubbing his palm over the back of his neck, he clenched his teeth. *Erica Fucking Lawson.*

His promising life as a Dom had been cruelly cut short by the dreaded *vanilla syndrome* and there seemed to be no cure for it in sight. *None what-so-fucking-ever.*

REDEMPTION

ELLA DOMINGUEZ

A Glimpse into Submission

An erotic journey of self-discovery where obsession and a yearning for control collide.

After a chance encounter brings a businessman face to face with an erotic set of paintings that were never intended to be sold, they rekindle a flame for the alternative lifestyle he was forced to give up. When he meets the shy artist, he hatches a wicked plan that will not only allow him access to more of her paintings, but to dominate and educate her in the ways of becoming his submissive. Faced with an offer that will permit her to explore her sexual desires—their passionate journey begins.

In spite of Dylan's trust issues and wanting only a physical relationship with distinct boundaries, their chemistry is powerful. Soon, he realizes that he can't resist Isabel's spirited nature, her eagerness and lack of fear to learn from him, and most of all—her immense talent.

But Isabel has a hidden dominant streak that only Dylan brings out, and despite being drawn to one another, their unexpected struggle for control and their dark pasts that are looming in the shadows, threatens to strip them of the fragile bond they so desperately cling to.

Warning: Contains erotic elements, BDSM themes, and situations that may trigger past memories of abuse. Intended for mature readers, aged 18+.

REDEMPTION

Submission: Chapter One
Dylan

A good fuck is precisely what Dylan needed. Not that a good fuck was something that was within reach, but a man could dream. Another dull day followed by another dull night had only solidified the fact that his sad vanilla routine seemed to have no end in sight. Despite that depressing fact, he was thankful he hadn't brought a date to the art exhibit so that he could get the hell out of there without any issues. The last thing he needed was the hassle of some social-climber on his arm pretending to enjoy his company, for any other purpose other than to be seen with him.

Why in Christ's name he had agreed to go to this particular gallery show was beyond him. He hated these things. He preferred viewing art at his own leisure. He preferred living life at his leisure too, but it seemed karma had other plans for him.

This is for charity and good for his public image, he reminded himself.

Surrounded by uninteresting, pretentious assholes that knew nothing about art and liked flashing their cash, he found himself nauseated by the overwhelming stench of cologne and perfume hanging in the air. He swore if he heard one more reference to Monet, he would lose his temper in spectacular fashion and really give the paparazzi something to write about.

They'd love that, too, wouldn't they? He could already read the headlines: *Businessman and art collector Dylan Young assaults innocent patrons. Claims: "I lost my shit."*

All the floral prints and bullshit happy images were too much. He had to get out of there, and damned fast.

REDEMPTION

As casually as possible, he circled around the gallery, trying to inch his way toward the door to make a hasty getaway, while hopefully avoiding the photographers. In his anxiousness to get out of Dodge, he momentarily got turned around and found himself in a dimly lit corner of the gallery. As he turned to get his bearings, he came face-to-face with three medium-sized canvases hanging inconspicuously on a darkened wall.

Though initially unable to decipher the lines and forms, he stopped dead in his tracks as his eyes scanned the deep shades of red and black interspersed among warm neutral hues throughout the paintings. When the imagery came into full clarity, the erotic and sinful subject matter thickened the blood in his veins and sent a flash of heat to his balls. As the images on the canvas seeped into his subconscious, the overwhelming urge to feel the cat o'nine tails in his hand and hear the sweet sound of leather lashing against flesh surged through him.

Though the imagery was fragmented, he understood it. It was *hard* not to. A lewd smile crept onto his face. It was *hard*—just like he was. More than that—the imagery spoke to him.

A burning curiosity to know who had painted his deepest desires forced his gaze to the corner of the painting. There he found the artist's name etched in white acrylic paint: *Isa.*

Dylan had never heard of him, and if he knew anything, he knew art. Seeing as the name wasn't a familiar one, he concluded it must be an unknown local artist.

A creeping sense of paranoia washed over him. *The artist had seen his dreams and knew of his past.* It was ridiculous to even entertain the thought, and Dylan knew it, but still, the uneasy feeling as if someone had peeked into his brain remained.

Unable to pull himself away from the paintings, an unannounced male gallery representative stealthily approached and interrupted his thoughts, making him jump.

"My apologies for startling you, Mr. Young. You seem to have lost your way, let me show you back to the main gallery," the sandy-blonde haired man remarked in a distinctively British accent.

The man was right—Dylan had lost his way, but there was no way in hell he was facing that mundane shit again.

"Thank you, but I'd much rather look at these paintings," Dylan commented blandly.

A look of shock flashed over the man's European features as his eyes flicked from Dylan to the paintings and then back again.

Patently ignoring the man's expression, Dylan continued. "Tell me about the artist who painted these."

"*Artist?*" he questioned, still clearly astounded at Dylan's interest in them. "I wouldn't say the person who painted these is an *artist*, per se."

Could the man be more condescending? Dylan doubted it. And what the fuck did he mean by that statement anyway? When the haughty asshole's look of surprise shifted to nervousness, Dylan could only assume it was from the cold hard stare he had thrust upon him.

Breaking the silence, Dylan plunged on, while ignoring the man's ambiguous comment. "This artist—is he local?"

Seemingly at a loss for words from Dylan's persistence in using the term *artist*, he answered, "No, he's not local. He's a bit shy and different. He's ..."

REDEMPTION

When he trailed off, Dylan finished his sentence for him.

"Eccentric?"

"A bit," the man stated with a nod.

And there it was—that word—*that thing*—that Dylan had been accused of being. Hell, he'd heard it so often and the term had been used so ubiquitously, it no longer held any meaning. It was merely a way for uninspired people to write off those who dared to be original.

"And very difficult to get a hold of," the man added. Although he'd said it as an afterthought, the look in his eyes led Dylan to think he meant something entirely different. He promptly chimed up again, almost apologetically, "I only placed these here to take up space. We had an unexpected sale today, and I needed to fill the wall."

Though Dylan found the explanation lame, he couldn't care less. At that moment, all he wanted was possession of the paintings.

"Speaking of unexpected sales, I'd like to purchase these."

The same look of astonishment on the gallery representative's face resurfaced, making Dylan wonder if the ostentatious bastard had no other expressions.

"These aren't for sale. I'm sure I can find something more suited to your tastes, if you'll just follow me this way," he stated with uncertainty.

The man turned away from the paintings, but Dylan held his ground. Clearly, this douchebag didn't know fuck all about his tastes because these were right up his alley. Dylan almost voiced that sentiment, but his *public image* once again popped into his head, forcing him to refrain.

Dylan narrowed his eyes. "I'm not interested in anything else in your gallery. I want *these*. How much?" he asked firmly.

When a look of irritation flashed over the man's face, in place of the normal expression of dumbfounded shock, Dylan struggled to prevent the words *welcome to my world, you pompous ass* from slipping past his lips Motionless and staring at him with the focused and uncompromising gaze of a hawk fixed on its prey, Dylan waited for an answer. When the man finally broke and gave him a price, he got the distinct impression the man thought he'd quoted a price so ridiculous that Dylan would balk at the sale or try to negotiate. But Dylan didn't do negotiation. And, quite frankly, what the man was asking was chump change as far as he was concerned, especially considering how alluring the pieces were. Hell, he would have paid double what the asshole had asked.

Without hesitation, Dylan agreed to the stated price and reached into his back pocket to fish out his wallet, causing the now, all-too-familiar look of dumbfounded shock to return. Barely able to keep himself from laughing out loud at the man's ridiculousness, Dylan rolled his eyes and strode out of the room to find the cashier.

With the sale finished and ownership of the paintings now assigned to him, Dylan decided to forego the usual protocol of having the artwork delivered to him. Not that protocol mattered to him anyway; he wasn't asking for permission. With the paintings paid for, waiting the standard two or three days' delivery time to get his hands on the artwork was unacceptable. In no uncertain terms, he stated that he would pull around back to pick them up. Not surprisingly, the dealer looked shocked once more.

REDEMPTION

Back home, Dylan carried his precious cargo inside and carefully placed them on a large side table in his office. Once again, he found himself lost in the paintings. He commanded his eyes to scan every centimeter of each canvas, making sure that no detail was missed. Only when he realized the late hour did he pry himself away from them to bathe and get ready for bed.

In the shower, he was left alone with his crude thoughts and memories of his darker days. Good old days, if you will; at least, good for him. The memory of the BDSM club he used to frequent; *most* of his submissives; his beloved dungeon with all the tools of torture that lay within its four walls and the scenes that took place there—those had been good days, indeed. *Fuck, he missed it.* But that life was over for him now. Not by his choice, unfortunately; but nonetheless, it was over, and pointless to dwell upon for any length of time.

Unable to sleep due to the images of the paintings that kept invading his thoughts, Dylan found himself back in his office, gazing at the artwork, in spite of the late hour. Leather cuffs on delicate wrists, rope-bound ankles, and a submissive pose, compelling in their simplicity. The last one, a nude girl posed in graceful acquiescence, left him wondering about the identity of the model. It also left him pondering about the artist and how he could know Dylan's deepest, darkest thoughts. The only logical conclusion was that the artist must be into the BD lifestyle. Only someone who was into BDSM as heavily as Dylan had once been could have painted images like this. It was the only thing that made any sense.

Frustrated by his newfound obsession for the paintings, Dylan rearranged and shuffled them around in an attempt to figure out their meaning—*if* there was any meaning to be had. Finally giving up, he placed one on the floor while the other two remained on the side table, and turned to return to bed. He allowed himself one last look before trying to get back to sleep, and a sudden realization hit him—the paintings were three pieces of an unfinished puzzle. But where and how could he get the other pieces? He wanted the other pieces—for his sanity, *he needed them.*

*

Isabel

Having faced another monotonous day followed by another uneventful night, Isa suffered a pang of disappointment at her lack of invitation to the charity gallery show. Such were the consequences of being a person deemed unworthy of invitations to important events. There was no point in pouting about it, even if getting to participate in the event in some small capacity while Real Artists and beautiful people mingled about would have been worth selling one of her kidneys.

With nothing else to do, she decided to paint. At least it would take her mind off of her dismal existence and her continued idiocy for having allowed her asshole boss, Mr. Greer, talk her into loaning him her paintings. Holy hell, she was in denial. And consciously so, making her self-loathing flare more hatefully than usual. That man hadn't *talked* her into it—he had *insisted* on it. Worse yet, he had threatened her with unemployment if she didn't comply with his unreasonable demand.

She tried to pretend as if she didn't know what Greer's problem was. Unfortunately, the nagging voice of antipathy wouldn't allow for such a luxury. He wanted in her panties. *Again.* But once had been more than enough for her. The memory of him in her apartment, on her, *in* her—sent shudders of repulsion creeping over her flesh. It was ironic, considering that had been the exact same reaction she'd had the first time she'd met him. The look in his eyes at her interview should've been unnerving enough to send her running in the opposite direction just as far and fast as her short legs would take her, but the temptation of working at an art gallery had been too much to resist.

What a colossal mess. As much as she missed sex, regardless of how boring it had been she vowed to stick with finger-banging herself rather than letting something that stupid happen again.

She refused to think about it any longer and pushed the wretched memory to the back of her mind. She wanted her property back. Cursing under her breath about her predicament, she vowed that she would demand her paintings back the following day. Or, maybe ask nicely—whichever method worked best.

The thought of strangers ogling her paintings made her stomach roil with anxiety. *What would people think of them?* That she was a freak, no doubt. And deep down, she had to agree. Regardless of what people thought, how dare that asshole Greer expect her to be okay with putting her precious artwork out there for the world to see? That would equate to asking someone to put pages of their diary up for show and tell. Her paintings, like personal journal pages, were her deepest, darkest longings—her filthy fantasy life played out on canvas.

It was her own damned fault. She never should have allowed him entry into her place when he had shown up uninvited that very first time. If she hadn't, he would never have seen her artwork, and she wouldn't be in this situation.

Giving up on the idea of getting anything satisfying on canvas, she threw herself onto her bed. As she lay there staring up at the wall where her paintings had once hung, mentally kicking herself, a plan of action began to formulate in her head. An innocent appearance at the show pretending like she'd forgotten her wallet suddenly seemed a viable, though pathetic, idea. She could then sneak a peek at where Mr. Insistent had put her paintings. She might as well take advantage of the circumstances, seeing as it would be the one and only time her art would *ever* be in a gallery.

She was in and out of the shower quickly and, despite the weather still being warm and fall being a good month away, she dressed in a pair of jeans and a sweatshirt. Not that she had much else to choose from seeing as she liked clothing that hid what she considered to be her less-than-appealing figure. She figured some men probably went for the short, curvy kind, though she hadn't met many, and certainly none that were worthwhile.

A quick glance in the mirror revealed her usual uncompromising hair, and attempts to tame it only proved futile. Reminding herself that there was no one to impress, she gave herself a final critical once-over before leaving.

The thirty-minute bus ride from her apartment to the studio left her feeling anxious, but it carried the benefit of being dropped off a block away from the gallery to ensure that Mr. Greer wouldn't see her. Slowly, she made her way across the street as she observed the festivities. Limousines, large pricey SUVs and a few exotic sports cars lined the street near the gallery. It was impressive. As much as she detested Mr.

REDEMPTION

Greer and his bitchy cohort, Monica, she had to give them credit for putting on one hell of a show.

Several people milling around near the main entrance, including security and a handful of photographers, paid her no mind as she peered from a distance into the large front windows. The scene beyond the glass was even more remarkable than the one out front.

She darted across the street as stealthily as possible to the front of the gallery. One peek past the glass revealed beautiful, seemingly flawless trophy wives and girlfriends, as well as a few mistresses, no doubt. All were dressed to the nines. But the real highlight was the handsome men in their finest attire on the arms of those gorgeous women.

One man in particular stood out from the rest—Denver's very own Golden Boy and most eligible bachelor, Dylan Young.

Isa wasn't so much surprised that he'd made it on the guest list as she was pleased that he had actually attended. Even with the distance between them, she could see his striking blue eyes and how they contrasted with his dark, espresso-brown hair. Tallish and lean, wearing a grey tailored suit, his appearance was nothing short of delicious. So delicious, in fact, she wondered what he tasted like.

The jacket he wore was unbuttoned and open, revealing a crisp white shirt and tie that matched the color of his eyes. One of his hands rested in the pocket of his blazer, while the other massaged the back of his neck. A look of irritation and boredom flitted across his rugged face, and Isa envisioned a myriad of naughty ways to cure his boredom.

The cool blast of air that blew past her did little to bring her out of her lust-induced trance, but she knew that standing gape-jawed while daydreaming about a handsome stranger as if she was some kind of crazed stalker couldn't be a good look on her, so she quickly pulled herself back to reality.

Making her way to the side of the gallery and around to the back entrance, anxiety coursed through her veins. She hoped, even prayed, that Mr. Greer didn't see her. Gripped by her fear of encountering him, she almost turned to leave, but decided instead to push forward, as her Not-So-Dear Old Dad would say and *man-up*.

The room was dark, and only the faint sounds of voices and mellow music could be heard from the main area. The scent of masculinity replaced the usual smell of the gallery, exciting Isa. Nearly stumbling, she found her way to the room where the lesser known artists' paintings were, but was halted by the sound of Mr. Greer's voice and one she didn't recognize. Irritation laced Greer's tone, making Isa smile. Though she couldn't make out the topic of conversation, the words "shy and eccentric" stood out. The words sounded strange, as she couldn't recall seeing any paintings of particular interest in that room.

Momentarily deterred, she retreated to the back office to bide her time. As soon as the voices subsided, she attempted to make her move, but was again stopped by shuffling and movement that sounded a lot like items being taken down and packed away.

Once the room quieted down, Isa immediately strode to the place where she'd seen Greer hang her paintings. Faced with an empty wall where her paintings *should be*, Isa stood motionless and confused. The space where her artwork had been hung now stared back at her, blank and mocking. A slow influx of panic began to flood her mind as her eyes darted around the room at the few paintings left in that area. Panic turned to anxiety when it finally hit her that her paintings were gone.

But to where? Surely someone hadn't bought them. The room was closed off from the show. Though she wanted to seek out Mr. Greer and ask him where he'd put her paintings, a sad realization came over her—perhaps Greer had decided her art wasn't good enough for even the not-so-relevant section. *Yes, that was it.* He'd simply taken them down because of their perverse nature and hidden them away.

Not wanting to risk getting caught, she decided to hold off asking about them until the following day at work.

Back home and in bed, Isa's imagination came alive, and her thoughts began to morph—just like they did every night. Comforted by the visions of wrist cuffs and rope that adorned contorted bodies being used in sinful and pleasurable ways, she closed her eyes and drifted off, fantasizing about the sound of a snapping whip. Those dark images and imagined sounds, no matter how perverse they might seem to someone else, were like a sweet lullaby to her.

Late in the night, she woke drenched in sweat, her pussy throbbing and soaking wet. She'd had an orgasm in her sleep. Or, at least she thought she'd had an orgasm. She wouldn't exactly know what one felt like, considering her sexual experience had been limited to selfish assholes that never cared whether or not she got off. From the get-go, her sex life had been utterly dull and unexciting, and from the looks of it, there was no hope for a cure.

She pushed a finger past her labia and touched her still tingling clit. Whatever had happened, it had been *nice.* With a gentle rub of her wrists, her vivid dream slowly slipped from her memory.

More from Ella Dominguez

Submission (The Art of D/s Rewritten, Book One)
*Domination (The Art of D/s Rewritten, Book Two)
*Control (The Art of D/s Rewritten, Book Three)
*Coming late 2017/From the previously titled Art of D/s series
Becoming Sir (An Art of D/s novel)

Continental Breakfast (Continental Affair #1)
Continental Beginnings (Continental Affair #2)
Continental Life (Continental Affair #3)
Continental Affair Series

This Love's not for Sale

Grace Street (Chapter 8, #1)
Return to Grace Street (Chapter 8, #2)
Chapter 8 Series

Altered State
Hard Candy for Christmas
The 12 Kinks of Christmas
A Cub for Christmas
F#ck You Valentine!

Adam's Apple: An Erotic Short Story

Ulterior Designs (House of Evans, Book One)
Interior Motives (House of Evans, Book Two) *Coming Soon

REDEMPTION

About Ella D.

Mother, lover, dreamer and someone with an unhealthy obsession with ukuleles and unicorns, Ella was born and raised in a conservative, strict Christian household in the Bible Belt of the USA. This upbringing and repression contributed to her wicked imagination, and writing has become a pleasurable and satisfying outlet for her fantasies. At the 'mature' age of forty, she mustered up the courage to share her thoughts and put pen to paper. She sincerely hopes to find her niche in writing romance in all forms, be it dark romance, romantic suspense, romantic comedy, psychological thrillers and paranormal.

She doesn't consider herself an author, rather, an avid reader above all else and someone who simply writes the stories that the characters in her head tell her to.

Website: www.bondagebunnypub.com

Newsletter: http://eepurl.com/bwsvUf

Blog: www.elladominguez.blogspot.com

facebook.com/theartofsubmission

twitter.com/ella_dominguez

goodreads.com/author/show/6472437.Ella_Dominguez

www.instagram.com/ella_dominguez/

Made in United States
Orlando, FL
15 June 2024